panda series

PANDA books are for young readers making their own way through books.

D1078921

O'BRIEN SERIES FOR YOUNG READERS

O'BRIEN panda cubs

O'BRIEN pandas

O'BRIEN panda legends

O'BRIEN flyers

Emma
the
Penguin

• SARAH WEBB •
Pictures by Anne O'Hara

THE O'BRIEN PRESS
DUBLIN

Dedicated to Emma Barton

First published 2010 by The O'Brien Press Ltd,
12 Terenure Road East, Dublin 6, Ireland.
Tel: +353 1 4923333; Fax: +353 1 4922777
E-mail: books@obrien.ie
Website: www.obrien.ie

ISBN: 978-1-84717-195-5

British Library Cataloguing-in-Publication Data
A catalogue reference for this title is available from the British Library.

The O'Brien Press receives assistance from

1 2 3 4 5 6 7 8 9 10
10 11 12 13 14 15

Typesetting, layout, editing, design: The O'Brien Press Ltd
Printed and bound by M&A Thomson Litho Ltd.
The paper in this book is produced using pulp from managed forests.

Can YOU spot the panda
hidden in the story?

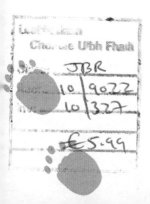

It was almost the end of term.
'We are going to do a play,'
said Miss Bird.
'It is *Noah's Ark.*'

The class cheered.
Emma was excited.
She loved plays.

Ruby Ryan put up her hand
and waved it about.

Ruby always put up her hand.
She always had something
to say.

'Yes, Ruby?' Miss Bird said.
'Can Noah be a girl, Miss?'
said Ruby.

Ruby wanted the main part.
Ruby always wanted
the main part.

Simon O'Reilly pulled a face.

'Don't be silly, Ruby.

Noah's a boy's name.'

Miss Bird frowned at him.

'Well,' said Miss Bird,

'a girl could play Noah.

But this time

I think we'll have a boy

for that part.'

'But,' Miss Bird said,
'Noah had a wife.
And she had three
daughters-in-law.
So there will be plenty of parts
for all the girls.
And there are lots of
animal parts, of course,
for everybody.'

All the children wanted to be
their favourite animal.
'Can I be a cat?'
Chloe asked.
'Can I be a dog?'
said Emma.

'Can I be a horse?'
said Olivia.
Olivia was Emma's best friend.
She was mad about horses.

'I'm going to be a shark,'
said Simon O'Reilly.
He stuck his hand
up from his head
and ran around
the classroom,
pretending to
eat people.

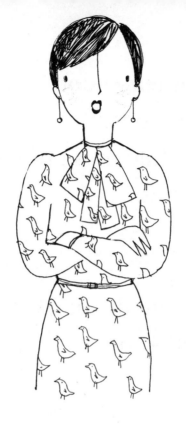

Miss Bird clapped her hands.

'Sit down please, Simon.

And settle down, class.

You'll all get parts, I promise.

But it will be done fairly.'

Later, after school,
Miss Bird put
all the children's names
in one hat.

She put all the parts
in another hat.

She pulled out a piece of paper
from each hat.

Each child had a part to play.

Next morning, Miss Bird
handed each child
their piece of paper.

Emma closed her eyes
and wished: DOG.
She opened her paper.

It said: **PENGUIN**.
OH NO!

'What did you get?' said Olivia.

'Penguin,' said Emma. 'You?'

'Cat,' said Olivia. 'I hate cats.'

'I'll swap with you,' said Emma.

'Nobody is allowed to swap,'
said Miss Bird.

Olivia was thinking.

'Maybe I could be
a **lucky** black cat,' she said.
'I could wear
my black ballet leotard
and black tights.
And I could wear
my black party shoes
with the silver sparkles.'

She started to smile.
'Maybe being a cat
is better than being a horse.'

Emma was thinking too.
But she couldn't think of
a single thing to wear
to be a penguin.

Her black boots?
No. Penguins have flippers, not feet.

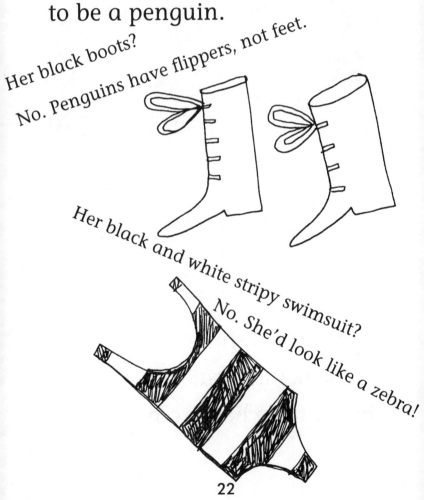

Her black and white stripy swimsuit?
No. She'd look like a zebra!

Emma was very sad.
What was she going to do?
Everyone talked about
their cool animal costumes
all day long.

Emma was **fed up**.

And guess who
the other penguin was!
Simon O'Reilly.

Then Miss Bird said
that the penguins
would have to do
a special waddle
up the gangplank of the ark,
to make people laugh.

Oh no!
It got **worse** and **worse**.

Olivia came to Emma's house
to play after school that day.

'Any news, girls?'
Emma's mum asked.
'No!' said Emma.
'Yes!' said Olivia.
'We're doing *Noah's Ark*
and I'm going to be a cat.'

'That's lovely, Olivia,'
said Emma's mum.
'And what are you
going to be, Emma?'

Emma said nothing.

'Emma's a penguin,'
Olivia said.
'But she's not
very happy about it,
are you, Emma?'

Emma said nothing.

'I'm sure you'll be
a great penguin,'
Emma's mum said.
'And I have a good idea
for a penguin costume.'

Long ago, Emma's mum
was a waitress in a posh hotel.
That night, she took out
her old uniform.
And she found a top hat
to go with it.

Emma stared at herself
in the mirror.
'I look silly,' she said.

Mum smiled.
'I think you look fantastic.'

'I don't want to look silly.
I don't want to
make people laugh,'
Emma said.
'Why can't I be like Ruby?
She gets to be Mrs Noah.'

'And Chloe
and Aoife and Gracie
are her daughters-in-law,'
said Emma.
'And they all get to sing.
And I get to be a
stupid old penguin.'

'You look great, love,'
said Mum.

For the next three weeks,
Miss Bird's class
practised and practised.

Every day, they
sang the *Noah's Ark* songs,
and did the *Noah's Ark* dances.

Even Emma began to enjoy it.
She started to **like**
being a penguin.

She and Simon had to
waddle up the gangplank.
They had to try to trip up
the other animals.

They had to sing the song
'Raindrops Keep Falling
on My Head'
and twirl big black umbrellas.

It was great fun.
Emma and Simon
were getting very good
at making people laugh.

Emma even began to like
her costume.

She even began
to like **Simon** (a little bit).
But she didn't tell anyone that!

The week before the play,
Miss Bird said:
'On Thursday, we will have
a full dress rehearsal
in the school hall.
Everyone must come to school
in their *Noah's Ark* costume.
Any questions?'

Ruby's hand shot up.

'Yes, Ruby?' said Miss Bird.

'Will we put make-up on?'
said Ruby.

'No, Ruby, just your costume,
no make-up.'

On Wednesday,
Emma woke up
with a sore throat.
Mum took her temperature.
'No school today,' Mum said.
'But if you stay in bed,
I think you'll be okay
tomorrow.'

Emma sipped hot lemon
and honey drinks all day.

That night she felt
much better.

Next morning
she jumped out of bed
and smiled at her
penguin costume.
She could feel a bubble of
excitement in her tummy.

And it wasn't
even the
real play yet!

She pulled on her costume,
and gobbled her breakfast.

'I must be quick
this morning,' Mum said.
'I have an important meeting.'
She dropped Emma off
at the school gate
and drove away.

Emma started to walk
towards the school door.
Ruby Ryan was in front of her,
in her **school uniform**.
That's funny, thought Emma.

'Hey, Ruby,
where's your **costume**?'
Emma shouted.

Ruby swung around.
'Emma! What are you
wearing?'

Emma spotted Olivia
in her school uniform.
Where was Olivia's
cat costume?

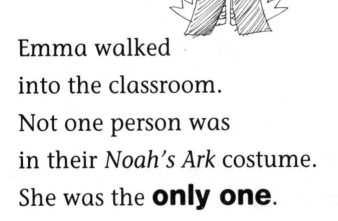

Emma walked
into the classroom.
Not one person was
in their *Noah's Ark* costume.
She was the **only one**.

Simon O'Reilly pointed at her
and started to laugh.

'Look at Emma.

She looks really stupid.

She looks like a **clown**.'

Miss Bird sighed.

'Oh, Emma, I'm so sorry.

There's a problem with

the roof of the school hall

and we're having the

dress rehearsal tomorrow.

I forgot to ring your mother.

If I call her now,

do you think she might pop in

with your uniform?'

'She has an
important meeting,'
Emma said.

Miss Bird nodded.
'Oh dear! Well, I suppose
you'll just have to be
a penguin for the day, Emma.
Great costume, by the way!'

By first break,
the whole school had heard
about Emma's mistake.

All the children
gathered around her
in the playground.

'What are you supposed to be?'
one little girl asked.
'A penguin,' Emma said,
wishing they'd all go away
and leave her alone.

'You don't look like a penguin,'
the little girl said.
'You look like a waiter.'

'When I have my
stage make-up on,
I'll look like a penguin,'
said Emma.

By the end of the day,
she was sick of the
bad penguin jokes.

What does a penguin wear
on rainy days? His **mac**kerel.

What do you call fifty penguins
on Grafton Street? **Lost**.

Why do penguins carry fish in their beaks?
Because they have **no pockets**.

At last, it was time
to go home.
It was Emma's
worst day ever.

And now she had to wait
outside the school gate
in her **penguin costume**.

'Go on,' said Simon O'Reilly.
'Give us a waddle,
clown-girl.'

Emma was very fed up.
Why not? she thought.
Why not make a fool
of myself?

'Do you still have
that cool song
on your mobile?'
she asked Olivia.

Olivia nodded
and turned it on.
Dance music rang out.

Emma started to waddle,
flapping her hands
like flippers.

Then she started to do
a funny little dance,
wiggling her bum
and shaking her shoulders.

Everyone started to laugh
and clap along with the music.

She rolled her eyes.

She puffed out
her cheeks.

She wobbled
her head.
She scrunched up
her shoulders.

When Emma finished,
everyone clapped and cheered.
The younger children
started to chant:
'**Penguin**, **penguin**,
penguin!'

'I'm sorry for teasing you,
Emma,' said Simon.
'We'll be the best penguins ever!'

Miss Bird rushed over to Emma.
'**Wonderful**!' she said.
'You must do that
in the play.
You'll be the
star of the show!'

And from that day on,
Emma loved making
people laugh.

She knew now that people were laughing **with** her, not **at** her.

Emma loved being
Emma – the clown.